# The Oracle

by Linda Hoy

Illustrated by Colin Hadley

# Contents

# CHAPTER 1

# Running Away

Running.

Heart pounding. Feet bounding. Running across the moor.

Panting.

The sky is black. Only a narrow band of moonlight glistens behind a cloud.

I leap across the rocks, feet pounding on the grass. Alone in the wilderness. No one to hear me.

Run. Run. Running.

My heart pounds: bam, bamba bam. Bampa bamp. Bam.

My feet hurt and my legs ache. I stop for a moment and listen.

Silence.

The silence of the moor unfolds like a huge grey blanket. Not a single sound.

I turn round and listen again.

Nothing.

Not even a bird or the scratch of a mouse. Just the empty moor stretching out before me, a huge, vast wilderness. And the only sound, the beating of my heart: bam. Bamba bam. Bampa bam. Bam.

I stand alone in the darkness; alone in the wilderness; alone in the moonlight on the moor.

I reach in my pocket and feel the stone.
Round and smooth.

I am running away with the stone. Taking
it back to the circle.

No one can stop me now.

I set off again.

Running.

I leap across the heather. Jump across the
rocks. The moon sparkles on the heather and
glistens on the ferns.

Soon I will be there.

# CHAPTER 2

# The Stone Circle

Tonight is a special night, the shortest night of the year.

Midsummer.

People come to the circle every year to celebrate. They call it the summer solstice.

Last year I came with Bob.

We drove here in Bob's old bus. It had beds and a place to cook. It had comfy chairs and tables. We parked in an old quarry. There were lots of other people. Lots of children and dogs. We all set off walking together to the stone circle across the moor. It was dark when we arrived. We lit a big bonfire and cooked potatoes and veggie burgers. Then we sat in a circle and ate the food while people

played drums and guitars. They played and
sang all night until the sun rose in the
morning. Then we all joined hands and
danced round in a circle. I thought it was
wonderful. Everyone was happy. I decided
there and then that I wanted to stay with Bob.
I wanted to live with him in the bus and travel
around. I didn't want to go back home.

When Bob did take me home, my mum was mad. Furious. "What sort of place is that to take your son?" she yelled at Bob. "A load of filthy hippies, staying out all night. Taking drugs and getting drunk. What kind of life is that?"

I hadn't seen anybody taking drugs. People just seemed to be having a good time. "I enjoyed it," I told her. "It was great."

"Well," Mum yelled at Bob, "that's the last time you take him out."

## Chapter 3

# Stone Skull

I pause again to get my breath. I can see more clearly now. The moon glints on the path and shines across the moor. I can see big rocks on the horizon and then the standing stones of the circle.

Not far now.

My heart is beating louder: bampa bam. Bampa bam. Bampa bam. My body aches. I feel exhausted, but I'll be at the circle soon.

I feel the stone in my pocket and remember Bob saying: "This is a very special stone. People would have used it a long, long time ago." He showed me where the stone had been axed in half. "You break the stone in two," he explained, "then you rub both halves together. After a while, it makes a spark. You place dry grass and twigs underneath so they catch fire. That's how people made fires long ago."

The stone fits neatly in my palm with three holes for my fingers. It looks like a skull with a hollow mouth and eyes. When we found the stone, Bob lit some incense and placed it inside. Then, it glowed like a burning skull with smoke curling out of its mouth.

# CHAPTER 4

# The Earth Shakes

I can see something.

I stand and peer into the distance. There's a reddish glow. A bonfire? My heart leaps with excitement. It must be the bonfire. Everyone will be there, joining in the celebration.

I leap forward.

I imagine Bob sitting by the fire with his friends. They'll be playing drums and guitars. He'll have such a surprise when he sees me.

I dash across the heather. I can see the light more clearly now. I can see shadows round it, flickering. I think I can hear a noise.

I stand still and listen: Bam bampa bam.
Bam bampa bam. The sound of my heartbeat.

Or is it?

There's another sound as well, a vibration
through the earth. A distant drumbeat. I
tingle with excitement. I've done it. I've found
the solstice celebration.

I leap forward.

Bampa bam. Bampa bam.

And wafting towards me on the breeze is
the smell of roasting meat.

A barbecue?

I start to run even faster.

Now I can see the stones. They seem taller than I remember. They glisten in the moonlight. I can see people as well, dancing round the circle.

The crowd is much bigger than it was last year. The earth shakes with the beating of drums and the stamping of hundreds of feet. I can hear voices – not singing but chanting. Like a noisy football crowd.

I hesitate. I don't recognize the words.

I peer through the darkness.

The dancers are huge. They're wearing massive headdresses like figures in a carnival. One has antlers like a giant stag; another a head like an eagle.

Perhaps it's a fancy dress party?

I'm not so sure.

I walk a bit more slowly.

How will I recognize Bob if he's wearing a strange mask?

I don't know.

Of course, I didn't tell Bob I was coming. He's not expecting me. But he'll recognize me when he sees me.

The smell of meat is stronger. I don't know what it is – chicken perhaps, or burgers? I'm a bit surprised because all the travellers I met with Bob were vegetarian. They didn't eat any meat.

And then there's another, sweeter smell. Like incense. Clouds of smoke swirl around the circle like a smoke machine at a concert.

Perhaps that's what it is – a rock band.

But why would they be playing in the middle of the moor? And why would they have only drums?

Then I hear a sound that makes me freeze.

# CHAPTER 5

# Sacrifice

A girl is crying.

Not a normal, quiet sobbing but the sound of someone in pain. She sounds very, very frightened. Her voice cries out above the drumbeat and the chanting. She sounds terrified. But the dancers carry on, pounding their feet on the ground. The drums carry on: Bam. Bampa. Bam bampa. Bam.

Nobody stops to help her.

Why not?

I stand and stare.

The girl is crying yet no one stops to see what's wrong with her.

My palms are sweating. I squeeze the stone tightly in my hand.

Something is wrong.

This is not a normal party. I don't think it's a concert either.

I step towards a large rock, then kneel down and peer over the top. No one can see me here. The dancers twirl round and round in the firelight. They're wearing masks and headdresses and some have paint on their faces. The girl is still crying in the middle of the circle but everyone dances round her.

I crouch behind the rock.

Bampa bam. Bampa bam. Bampa bam.

The voices chant louder. The dancers twirl. The earth trembles with their stamping.

The girl screams.

I think I ought to go back. I peer over the rock, and this time I can see the girl. She's standing on a large table or a kind of stage. Her hands are tied. She's struggling. She has long red hair, reaching nearly to her waist and she's wearing a long white dress.

The drums beat louder. Voices shout. Then a big cheer. Something else is happening. A procession. A line of men with spears raised. They march through the crowd. The last man is very tall with an enormous headdress like a stag. Everyone cheers when they see him. He turns and clambers onto the stage. His face is painted red with black rings around his eyes. The stag's head he wears has huge, curled antlers. He stands behind the girl. The drums stop. The crowd becomes silent.

I clamber to my feet. I stand, rigid with fear.

Everyone's eyes are fixed on the figure standing in the centre of the stage. There's silence as he speaks.

My heart beats like a drum, not with exhaustion now, but fear. I grip tightly to the stone, still wrapped in the palm of my hand. Sweat runs down my back.

The man talks to the crowd. His voice rises with emotion. The people shift restlessly. Lone voices shout in anger. People wave flame torches in the air.

The man speaks louder.

The girl screams.

Suddenly, the crowd lets out a cheer. People begin stamping on the ground. They beat a different rhythm: bampa bamp bamp bam. Bamp bamp bamp bam. The girl screams again. She's terrified. I can see her struggling but she seems to be tied up. I don't

think she can escape. The man raises his spear high in the air and the crowd lets out another yell. I find myself stumbling forward. I don't know what I'm thinking I might do. A voice shouts out. "Stop it!" It's my voice. "Leave her alone!" I yell.

I stagger forwards across the grass. "Stop it!" I shout again.

The man pauses with his spear held high. He looks towards me. I don't know if he can see me in the dark.

"Leave her alone!"

I run towards him. I don't know what I'm going to do, but my feet have a life of their own. They run and jump across the heather. Run and leap and run and ...

... then I stub my toe on a stone. I fall. I scream as I hit the ground. The last thing I hear is the strangled cry of the dying girl. Her voice mingles with my scream. I remember nothing else. My head hits hard rock as I fall ...

# CHAPTER 6

# Special Magic

It seems a long time before I open my eyes again.

I don't know where I am and I can't remember what's happened.

My nostrils quiver with the scent of grass and heather. I seem to be outside, lying on the ground.

Have I gone camping? Fallen asleep on a picnic?

I seem to remember something about a barbecue, but the picture I have in my mind is something scary.

What is it? What could possibly be scary about a summer barbecue?

When I try to concentrate, the picture melts away.

Someone is stroking my head. The touch is warm and soothing. I close my eyes again. I could just go back to sleep right here on the grass.

"Are you all right?"

Gentle. Soothing. A girl's voice, whispering in my ear.

A pleasant scent of herbs and soothing ointment. My head is being bathed gently with a perfumed, dampened cloth. The girl strokes my head with a touch as gentle as a butterfly's wing.

"Mmm ... ?"

I open my eyes.

At first, I'm dazzled by the golden glow of sunrise. The sun's rays shine and sparkle on the grass. Straight ahead of me lies a familiar circle of stone.

I remember Bob telling me about the stone circle on the moor. "It was built to catch the sunrise on the midsummer solstice," he explained. "That's the time of special magic, the turning of the year."

"Are you feeling any better?"

I turn towards the voice. Sitting beside me is a girl. She looks about my age. But that's where the likeness ends. Her long, red hair flows almost down to her waist. Her skin is dark brown and smooth, her eyes a sparkling green. She is very, very beautiful.

I blink.

The girl is dressed in a long, white robe covered with rich patterns of swirls and circles, beautiful birds and butterflies. She wears a golden necklace shaped like a long, coiled serpent.

I gaze into her eyes.

She smiles.

As we gaze at each other, it's as though
I'm meeting up with a long-lost friend, as
if I knew her once a long, long time ago.
I struggle to remember but my mind is
blank. There is a picture, but before I
can reach out and grasp it, it begins to melt
away.

I open my mouth. "Where am I?"

"Out on the moor. You fell."

I don't remember.

"Here. Drink this." She holds a cup to my
lips. Her fingers are clustered with rings, her
forearms painted with swirls and circles like
ornate dark tattoos.

I drink. The taste is bitter. I pull a face.

"Try and drink. It'll make you feel better."

I hold the cup and sip. Not a normal cup,
but a gold, carved goblet. More like a sports
trophy.

The girl smiles. "When you've finished your drink, you can start to tell me your story ..."

I sip the bitter drink and my mind begins to clear. It goes back to yesterday: the argument; the shouting.

"What were you doing on the moor?"

I sip some more. "Looking for my father."

The girl nods. "Why was that?"

I start to tell the girl about my dad ...

# CHAPTER 7

# Torn in Half

The girl listens as I talk about my father.

"He was an artist. He drew pictures for books and magazines. He used to make up stories especially for me, then he made little books for me with the stories in, and pictures. He was really clever. He made lots of money. Mum had a job as well. She worked in a bank, so we were quite well off. We had a big house in the countryside with a lovely garden and some hens. We were happy. Everything was fine until Dad lost his job."

The girl nods. She sits beside me, holding the golden goblet, saying nothing.

I carry on. "Dad tried and tried to find another job. He replied to adverts in the

newspaper; he sent his pictures off to different magazines; but nobody wanted his work. After a whole year without a job, he started feeling more and more depressed. He stayed in bed late every morning. When he did get up, he just walked to the pub in the village and stayed there most of the day."

I pick up my stone from the grass and cradle it in my palm.

"I really wanted to help my dad. I tried painting pictures and asking him to help. I even painted a mural on the hen house, hoping he might pick up a brush and show me how to do it. He never did. Then, after my baby sister was born, he began to drink more and more. Mum got mad with him and they started having rows. Mum had to pay someone else to look after the baby while she was at work because Dad was always too drunk. And when Mum came home, she had to clean the house, do the shopping and make the tea. The more angry she got with Dad, the more time he spent at the pub."

The girl passes the cup to my lips and I take another sip.

"In the end, Mum started going out with someone else – her boss at work. His name was Tom." I shake my head. "I hated him. I thought she should have waited longer and given Dad a better chance.

"Anyway, one day Mum packed all our things in cases. Tom drove round while Dad was at the pub and started loading our cases into his car. I cried. I didn't want to go. I hid in the hen house and closed the door and crawled under the straw with all the hens. They couldn't find me for ages. Tom got really mad. Then I heard Mum saying she was going to call the police. That's when I ran out of the hen house and they saw me. Tom had to drag me screaming to his car. I loved my Dad and I didn't want to leave him. I just wanted us all to stay together and be happy.

"Last summer, Dad asked if I wanted to stay with him for a week. After a lot of arguments, Mum and Tom agreed and Dad came to fetch me in his bus. You could sleep in the bus. I thought it was great. My dad looked different. He'd grown his hair long and grown a beard and wore lots of earrings and tattoos. He'd joined this group of travellers who drive around together in old vans and buses, and go to festivals and celebrate the solstice. None of them had proper jobs, but no one minded. It was like being on holiday all the time. I thought it was great. I wanted to live like that.

"When I got home, I explained to Mum and Tom that I didn't want to stay at school and take all my exams. I wanted to go and live with Bob and travel in the bus."

The girl shakes her head. "And they wouldn't let you go ... ?"

"My mum went mad. She said Dad was a hippie and a drunk and not fit to look after me. They talked about sending me away to boarding school. I didn't want to go. I wanted to live on the bus. What made me really mad was that Mum and Tom decided to get married. That meant that Tom could legally adopt me and become my father."

I gaze at my special stone and cradle it in my palm. "When we went to the summer solstice, Bob gave me this stone. It's a flint stone." I run my finger along the scar where it was axed in two. "It's special for me because I feel just like the stone – I feel torn in half.

"I feel torn in half because I had to leave my father. I feel torn in half when Tom buys me expensive presents like a new bike and a computer. Bob – Dad – couldn't afford to buy me anything like that. I feel torn in half when Tom asks me to call him 'Dad'. He's not my father. He never will be."

"And that's why you ran away ..."

I nod.

## CHAPTER 8

# Sibyl's Story

I gaze at the rising sun, lighting the stone circle as the girl wraps her dress around her knees. Her red hair tumbles round her shoulders and glints in the sunlight.

"My name is Sibyl."

I nod.

"I used to live here." Her gaze sweeps round the panorama of countryside.

I stare, puzzled. "But nobody lives up here. There aren't any houses. There aren't even any roads." I think for a few seconds. "There isn't even any water, is there?"

Sibyl smiles. "I lived a long, long time ago. A long time before you were born. In those days this was mostly forest. We cut down the trees and used them to build our homes. There was a road," she points, "just over there. And a lake. And a temple ..." she points towards the standing stones "... over there."

I find this very hard to believe. As I say, the girl seems only about my age.

"So," she carries on, "my name is Sibyl. My mother's name was also Sibyl. She was a medicine woman. You might have called her a witch."

A witch?

I say nothing.

"My mother taught me all her skills. She taught me which herbs to pick and how to mix them to make potions and medicines for healing."

"Was that what you used to bathe my head?"

She nods.

"My mother taught me the sacred songs and stories which her mother had taught her before. Stories about the goddesses. Stories and songs about animals and about the seasons: spring and summer, autumn and winter. She taught me how to make fire. She taught me how to make fire for cooking and for sacrifice."

"Sacrifice?" I gulp.

"At every harvest we had to offer sacrifices to the goddess. We offered sacrifices to the rain goddess when the earth was dry."

"Oh."

"The most important thing my mother taught me was to listen. People would travel miles and miles to seek advice. They would arrive at the temple and bathe in the sacred pool. Then they would sit in the temple and tell their story to the listening stone. It was my job to listen to the thoughts of the stone and speak its thoughts out loud."

"A listening stone? I'm sorry, but I've never even heard of a ..."

The girl smiles. She reaches into the pocket of her dress and pulls out a stone.

I gasp.

The stone is a dark, shiny flint stone shaped like a skull. It has deep empty eye sockets, a gaping mouth and a slanting, broken nose. The stone is almost identical to mine.

"Where did you find that?"

Sibyl reaches her stone towards mine and slides the two halves side by side. They fit together like pieces of a jigsaw. "It's not where I found my half," she smiles, "but where you found yours. That's the mystery."

"But my stone was here inside the circle."

Sibyl nods. She says nothing.

"So, what happened to you and your stone?"

Sibyl gazes sadly towards the rising sun, glinting on the stone circle. "It's a long, sad story ..." she begins.

# Chapter 9

# Invasion

The two halves of the stone lie together on the grass as Sibyl starts to tell her story.

"I lived here with my tribe. My mother was the high priestess, so I was to be the next priestess after her. That meant I didn't work on the land like other girls. My hands were soft and clean. I spent my time learning songs and stories. I practised mixing potions of medicine so I could become a great healer like my mother. I felt the same as you," she smiles. "I was happy. Happy with my home. Happy with my people. I had everything I wanted."

"And then what happened?"

Sibyl shakes her head sadly. "The invaders came."

"Invaders?"

"The Suddi. Invaders from the south. Men with weapons. Men with shields. Men with pointed spears." She shudders. "Men who tried to take our land.

"My people were not warriors but we refused to give up our land. This was the land where our grandmothers and their mothers before them were buried. This was the place of the temple and the sacred listening stone. It was our duty to protect it.

"So, we fought fierce battles with the Suddi. We fought only with sticks and fire and axes. We had no sharpened spears. But we did have sharp brains. We dug great pits at night and covered them with leaves and branches. The Suddi fell in them and died. After a while, the invaders gave up and went away. We held great celebrations.

"But then they returned with more men and more weapons. They returned with more anger and fury. The battles went on and on.

"In only a few months, many, many people died. The leaders of both tribes spent many hours talking until a peace plan was prepared. We agreed to trade peacefully. We agreed to let the Suddi pass through our land whenever they wished."

She pauses. "And there was to be a marriage. The leader of the Suddi had a son. He was to take for his wife the daughter of our high priestess."

"But that was you ... ?"

Sibyl nods.

"My mother came back from the peace conference and told me that, within four weeks, I was to be married – to the son of our greatest enemy."

# CHAPTER 10

# The Party

Sibyl turns to me and smiles. "What do you think I did when they said I had to be married ... ?"

"Hid in the hen house ... ?"

She grins and shakes her head. "I didn't want to leave my tribe, but when the wedding celebrations started, I began to feel excited. There was a huge feast. Everyone from both tribes was invited. It was to be the biggest party ever. I was dressed in beautiful clothes with gold jewels. Our two families gave each other expensive gifts. I thought our marriage would mean that both our tribes would now live in peace for ever.

"The party continued for four days and nights with music and lots to eat and drink." Sibyl smiles. "I was happy. Happy, that is, until I had to say goodbye to my mother. I thought, like you, that they'd have to drag me screaming from her. But of course, a queen – even a young one – is not supposed to scream out loud. A queen should always act with pride."

There's a sudden picture in my mind. The picture of a young girl, terrified and screaming. A girl tied up and held captive on a large table or a stage. "But what about ... ?"

"Mmm ... ?"

But as soon as I try to focus, as soon as I try to put the scene into words, the picture melts away and vanishes.

"Nothing. It doesn't matter." I shake my head. "Carry on."

"I thought I would soon be able to visit my mother again. I thought that, after only a few months, I would be sitting inside my mother's hut, describing all the different sights I had seen: mountains, temples and beautiful scenery. Things didn't turn out that way."

# CHAPTER 11

# The Land of the Suddi

Sibyl continues her story.

"Our journey lasted many days and nights. I didn't know the Earth was so vast. I was expecting any day that our horses would reach the end of the Earth and fall off. Then when at last we reached the land of the Suddi ..." Sibyl shakes her head, "... everything was bleak. For mile after mile, the land had been destroyed. They had burnt down forests. Cut down trees. *'Where will the birds nest now?'* I asked. *'Which birds will sing to wake us in the morning now you have destroyed their trees?'*

"No one could answer me.

"When we reached the village where my new husband lived, everything was dirty. There was rubbish everywhere. The path smelled of rotting meat. There was no one to clean up. No one bothered.

"The first night, we were invited to a great feast. I felt exhausted after the journey and would rather have slept. Instead I sat at the table with my husband and ate the new, strange food while he became more and more drunk.

"The following night, there was another feast. And the next night. And the next. They ate more food in one week than a whole family could eat in a month. And sleeping outside in the cold were children of their own tribe, starving. My husband's family refused to give them even their leftover bones. Every night they feasted until they were sick. They drank wine until they could move no more. Their manners were rude."

"Did they speak the same language as you?"

"No. Their words were strange and ugly. I had learnt a few words from my husband but, after I arrived, I chose not to learn any more. Of course, then I was lonely. I had no one to talk to. I cried every night for my family.

"But that was not the main problem. I had taken my basket of herbs and potions with me but, when my husband saw them he kicked the basket away. *'Witchcraft!'* he shouted. *'We'll have no witches here!'*

"The following week, I saw a big crowd in the market place. A woman was being held prisoner. I recognized her. She came from one of the tribes in the north. Like me, she was a priestess. An angry mob was dancing round her chanting: *'Witch! Witch! Burn the Witch!'*"

Sibyl shook her head in horror. "I couldn't believe it. *'What are they going to do?'* I asked my husband.

"'*Burn her,*' he told me. *'That's what we do with witches here. You'd best be careful.*'

"Of course, I couldn't stay to watch. I ran back home and wrote a letter to my mother.

I cannot bear to live here any longer. Please, please come and take me home.

"I sealed the letter and gave it to a messenger. I told him to keep the letter secret and bring me the reply. I waited many weeks. When the reply came, it said simply:

Wait.
Wait until the time is right.
Be patient.

Sibyl shakes her head in dismay. "*Patient!* How could I be patient, living in a land of savages? How could I live with men who cut down trees, destroyed the land and burned a holy priestess?

"I waited three more months, then wrote to my mother again:

> I cannot bear to live here
> any longer.
> Please, please come and
> take me home.
> I will die if I have to stay here.

"I did not have to wait long this time. The reply came in less than a week:

> You are my daughter. You will always be my daughter. Nothing can ever change that. But you must keep your loyalty inside. Intact. Strong and sturdy like a stone. They can move your body and take away your name but they cannot change who you are. Be patient. We will be together. When the time is right, the two of us will be united.

"And did you wait?"

Sibyl shakes her head again. "I decided my mother was stupid. I thought I knew better. I had to leave."

# Chapter 12

# Sorcery

Sibyl sips from the golden goblet before she continues with her story.

"I was angry with my husband. He could take my herbs away but not my skill. No one could stop me going out on the moor and finding more herbs and roots. Even as a stranger living in a strange land, I could still find everything I needed."

"Everything for what?"

"A sleeping potion. Seeds of the poppy. Toadstools. Tree bark. I ground them all together. Unfortunately ..." Sibyl shakes her head, "... the Suddi are large people, much taller than our tribe. My husband was a very big man and so I ..."

"What?"

"Well, it seemed a good idea to increase the dose. I was afraid he would wake up too soon, before I had left, so I gave him double."

"Wasn't that right?"

Sibyl shakes her head. "I forgot about the wine. I was wrong to mix a sleeping potion with such strong wine. Especially as he drank such a large amount."

"Did he sleep for a long time, then?"

Sibyl gazes across to the circle where the sun's rays now shine on all the standing stones. "He is still asleep."

I'm not sure at first what she means. "You don't mean ... ?"

"He was a savage!" she cries.

"So, anyway, I had to leave very quickly. I packed few belongings: my listening stone, a cloak, some bread and water. Then I took a horse and sped out across the moor. I thought I would soon find my way home. But I

became lost. Then before very long, there were bands of men on horses, searching across the moor. I raced and raced but they knew the way better than me. I could hear them getting closer. I thought I had escaped when I saw the temple of my village standing against the sky. But that was when the Suddi caught me – just before I reached my home."

There's silence.

"When they found my listening stone, they thought I used it to put spells on people. They thought that was how I killed my husband. They said the stone must be destroyed. They axed the stone in two and threw one half away. I grabbed the other half of the stone and pressed it with my fingers."

There was a long pause. Sibyl stares into space. Her eyes grow wide as though she's staring at a picture.

"As the fire became hotter, the stone glowed red and yellow. I held it in my hand and squeezed as I felt my life blood melt away. As my spirit left my body, I spoke to the stone. Instead of listening, I gave the stone my thoughts." She holds the stone tightly. "No one else has heard my thoughts before, for the stone was buried with me."

"Buried? But I thought you were ... I mean, I thought you were saying you were ... ?"

She nods. "Burnt, yes. They burned me. But they were still afraid of my magic. Afraid of what they called my witchcraft. They burned my body then dug a pit. They threw my remains inside, then filled it with earth and built a high tower with a turret all around.

"A few weeks later, when the Suddi had left, my mother returned to my grave. My soul heard her cry across the moor. Her voice had woken my spirit. My body was burned but no one can destroy your soul. I could still hear the voice of my mother crying for me."

I listened.

"My mother was searching for the other half of the stone. For many days and nights, she wandered across the moor, crying. When

she found the stone, she carried it to the tower. Then she placed it in the centre of my grave. I heard her speaking through the stone.

"She said: *'Sibyl, my daughter, who lies beneath the earth, I place this stone to mark the centre of your grave. Even though your body has been burned, your soul will still exist. It will live for ever as the Oracle – the listening stone. On the night of the summer solstice, when someone picks up the stone, your soul will return to hear their thoughts and speak the thoughts of the stone once more.'*

"Over the centuries, the soil moved. It covered the steep sides of the tower so that all that was left was the turret.

"And when people saw the turret sticking from the ground, they thought it was a stone circle. They didn't know it was a tower." Sibyl pauses. "And my grave."

## CHAPTER 13

# Ghost

I feel a cold chill trickling down my spine.

Does all this mean that Sibyl is a ghost?

The hair on the back of my neck begins to tingle.

Can I really be alone on the moor with a girl who's been dead two thousand years? A girl who's been burned as a witch?

Sibyl turns and smiles at me. She doesn't look dead. She looks just as beautiful as when I first saw her.

"Remember," she tells me, "that you are the son of your father. Nothing can ever change that. They can move your body and change your name but they cannot change who you are."

I gaze at the stone circle, searching for any signs of the solstice celebrations.

The circle is empty.

"Remember the words of my mother: *'Be patient. Wait until the time is right.'* "

There are no travellers. No camp fire. No smoke. It looks as though no one has been here for a long, long time. The travellers must have gone somewhere else this year.

And of course there is no sign of my dad.

"Even if you don't see your father for a while, you are still his son. There are times when you have to keep your loyalty inside, intact. Strong and sturdy as a stone."

Sibyl holds her half of the stone outstretched in the palm of her hand.

There's a long pause. I take a deep breath as I listen.

"Remember my words. I am Sibyl. The Oracle. Do not forget my name."

I pick up the other half of the stone and cradle it in my palm. For a second or two it glows. Brighter than a star. Then I look up. The morning sun is dazzling. Perhaps it's just the sunlight shining on the stone.

Perhaps it's time for me to go.

I turn to speak to Sibyl but now there is no one there. I gasp. I turn around quickly. Just the empty moor stretching out as far as I can see. I turn again, searching. "Sibyl?"

No reply.

I am left alone.

"Sibyl?"

No answer.

I stand up. Something important has happened. Something I cannot understand.

My legs are shaky as I stand and gaze round the empty wilderness. I squeeze the stone in my palm and shout as loudly as I can. "Sibyl!"

For a second, there is nothing, then I hear a faint, far, trembling voice. An echo. "Sibyl!" Perhaps it is my voice echoing round the stones. Then I feel the icy tremor tingle once more down my spine. It doesn't sound like my voice. More like the voice of an old woman. I feel my palms damp with cold sweat as I remember Sibyl's story and imagine her mother, wandering over the moor, crying for her lost child, searching for the stone.

I pause. My eyes search again, but there is no one there. Only the standing stones and the sunlight, the dawn of midsummer day.

I look down at my feet for the other half of the stone but, just like Sibyl, it too has disappeared.

I know what I have to do. I must take my stone back home. I am older now and wiser. Even though I have only half of the stone, I now know the other half exists somewhere.

Mum and Tom will be worried about me, wondering where I am. Perhaps I ought to stop somewhere and phone.

I place the stone in my pocket.

I gaze at the standing stones once more, then start the long walk home.